Let's make rabbits

a fable by Leo Lionni

Dragonfly Books ———► *New York*

"Good morning," said the scissors
 to the pencil. "What shall we do today?"
"Let's make rabbits," said the pencil.

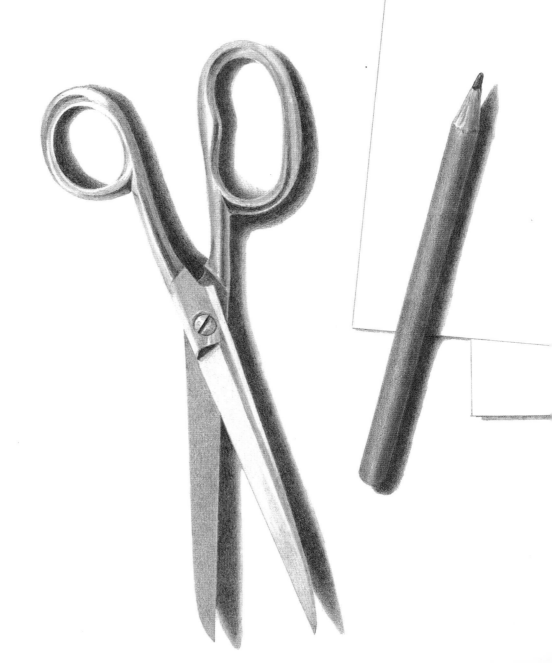

So they went to work. . . . The pencil drew a rabbit.

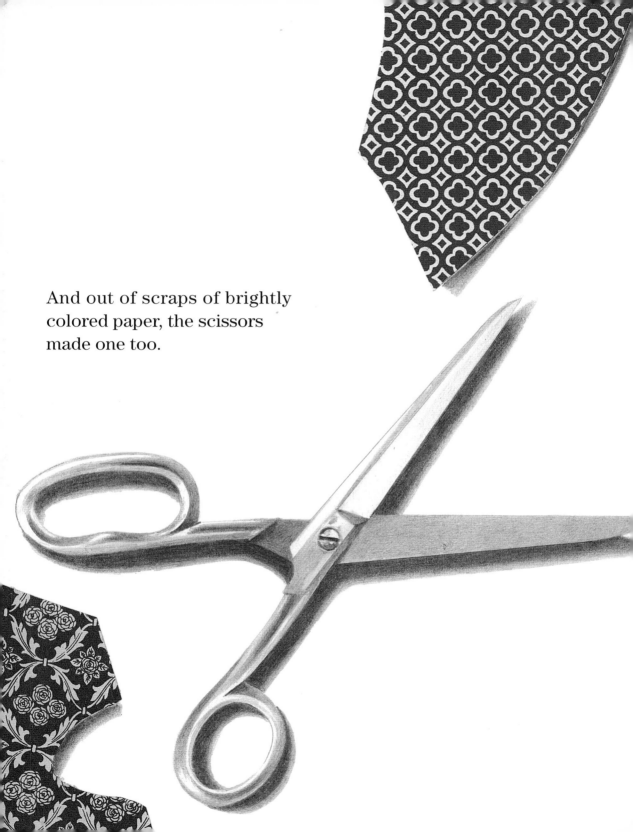

And out of scraps of brightly colored paper, the scissors made one too.

Immediately the two rabbits

were the best of friends.

But it wasn't long before they were hungry.

After looking in vain for something to eat,
they called the pencil and the scissors.
"We're hungry," they said.

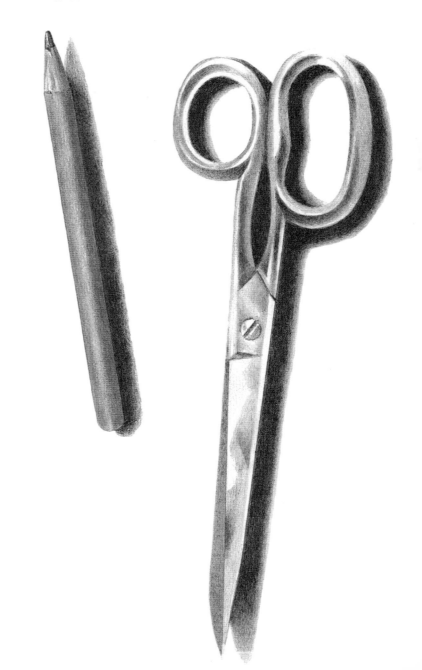

So the pencil drew a carrot,
and the scissors made one too.

The rabbits ate the carrots with joy.

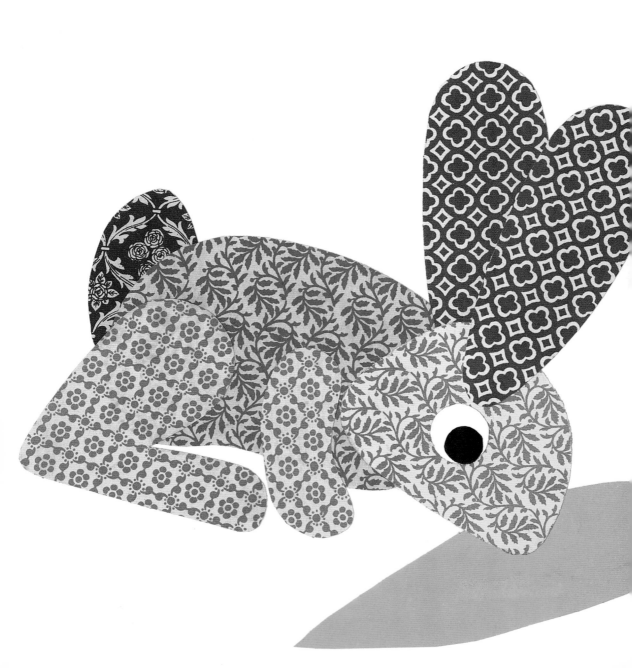

And then, with their tummies full,

they went to sleep.

When they woke up,
they were hungry again.

And again they called
the pencil and the scissors.

But this time no one came. They looked all over,
even outside the page . . .

. . . till suddenly they saw a big orange carrot.

"That carrot is *real*!" said the scissors rabbit.
"How do you know?" asked the pencil rabbit.
"It has a *shadow*!" the scissors rabbit replied.

"We'll eat it anyway," the hungry rabbits decided.

They sank their teeth into the tasty carrot,
and in no time it had disappeared, greens and all.

"Look!" said the pencil rabbit.
"Look! We have shadows too."
"We are *real*!" they both exclaimed.

And happily they hopped away.

About the Author

Leo Lionni, an internationally known designer, illustrator, and graphic artist, was born in Holland and studied in Italy until he came to the United States in 1939. He was the recipient of the 1984 American Institute of Graphic Arts Gold Medal and was honored posthumously in 2007 with the Society of Illustrators Lifetime Achievement Award. His picture books are distinguished by their enduring moral themes, graphic simplicity, and brilliant use of collage, and include four Caldecott Honor Books: *Inch by Inch*, *Frederick*, *Swimmy*, and *Alexander and the Wind-Up Mouse*. Hailed as "a master of the simple fable" by the *Chicago Tribune*, he died in 1999 at the age of 89.

Copyright © 1982 by Leo Lionni

All rights reserved. Published in the United States by Dragonfly Books, an imprint of Random House Children's Books, a division of Random House, Inc., New York. Originally published in hardcover in the United States by Pantheon Books, a division of Random House, Inc., New York, in 1982.

Dragonfly Books with the colophon is a registered trademark of Random House, Inc.

Visit us on the Web! www.randomhouse.com/kids

Educators and librarians, for a variety of teaching tools, visit us at www.randomhouse.com/teachers

The Library of Congress has cataloged the hardcover edition of this work as follows:
Lionni, Leo.
Let's make rabbits.
Summary: Two rabbits made with a pencil and scissors become real after eating a real carrot.
[1. Rabbits—Fiction.] I. Title. PZ7.L6634Le   [E] 81018713
ISBN 978-0-394-85196-9 (trade) — ISBN 978-0-394-95196-6 (lib. bdg.)

ISBN 978-0-679-84019-0 (pbk.)

MANUFACTURED IN CHINA
11 10 9 8 7 6 5 4 3 2